christmas 2013

PRAYERS
FOR
CHILDREN

our very special
grandchildren

with love
XOXO

Poppa & gramie

The sky's the limit!

At Sunshine Meadows the sky's the limit when it comes to a child's potential. It's a place where the never ending journey of learning begins and imagination soars, inspiring children to dream about all that they can be.

www.sunshinemeadows.com

Sunshine Meadows LLC
Published by Professor Harold
2065 Flamingo Drive
Costa Mesa, CA 92626

Design and illustration: Hugh Dunnahoe, Dunnahoe Creative Arts

ISBN-13: 978-1461019756
ISBN-10: 1461019753

Library of Congress Cataloging-in-Publication Data is available.

PRAYERS
FOR
CHILDREN

Written by Oh! Suzannah

Illustrated by Hugh Dunnahoe

Created by Oh! Suzannah and Harold Weitzberg

SUNSHINE MEADOWS

A Smile of a Child

Hear ye a saying ancient and old

All guardian angels are told

God's children are treasures

To love and behold

For a smile of a child

Is more precious than gold

My Wonderful World

Lord, I thank you for the world.
It's a really cool place!
There are trees, grass, and water,
And even outer space.
Bugs and birds, and animals
Are fun to find and see.
Thanks for making my world
A wonderful place to be.

Amen

Manners

Lord, please help me mind my manners.
I need them every day.
Sometimes it isn't easy knowing
What to do and say.
And help me not to slurp and burp
In the middle of my meal.
At home, a party, or at school,
Manners are a really big deal!

Amen

Safety

The safest way I can cross the street
Is to stop and look each way.
Wearing a helmet while riding a bike
Protects my head at play.
Tying my shoes so I won't fall
Is a very smart thing to do.
Carefully aiming when throwing a ball
Keeps me from trouble, too.
Lord, help me to think about safety first,
Not only just for me,
But also to care about those I love,
My friends and family.

Amen

Education

Getting a good education is one
Of the best things I can do.
Preparation and determination
Will help make a dream come true.
It seems I can do anything
If I'll only just believe.
Lord, bless me as I go to school
And work hard to achieve.

Amen

My Amazing Brain

Lord, thank you for my amazing brain.
It helps me learn most anything,
Like riding a bike or tying a shoe,
Reading and writing and telling time, too.
I know it weighs, my teacher said,
About three pounds inside my head.
It helps me walk, talk, know, and see.
God, bless my brain and,
God, bless me.

Amen

Be a Friend

Lord, I know it's good to listen,
To know what others need.
Please help me not to think about
What's only good for me.
I need good ears to listen with,
So everywhere I go,
People will see I can be
A very good friend to know.

Amen

One of a Kind

Lord, it's great to know I'm one of a kind,
That I'm the only me.
Please open my eyes and help me see
All I'm meant to do and be.
I could become a scientist, a doctor,
Or a trainer in a zoo.
Maybe I'll travel around the world
And sail the ocean blue.
Thank you, Lord, for helping me be
The one, and only, incredible me.

   Amen

A Can-Do Attitude

Lord, help me to discover,
In everything I do,
How a can-do attitude can
Really help me through.
Whether I'm doing chores, studying,
Or having fun at play,
I can choose a can-do attitude
And have a happy day.

Amen

You've got Talent

Lord, I know you made me special,
With talents I can share.
Teach me how to use them
In ways that show I care.
And help me see the talents
In other people, too.
Whether painter, singer, or athlete,
All talent comes from you.

Amen

Helping Hands

Lord, sometimes when I help others
It makes me feel good, too.
Taking out trash or raking leaves
Are a few things I can do.
What I really like to help with,
In case you want to know,
Is mixing yummy chocolate chips
In gooey cookie dough.
But help me to remember, Lord,
Wherever my path leads,
My helping hands can look for ways
To meet needs with good deeds.

Amen

Dream Big

I have big dreams about my future, Lord.
There's so much I want to do.
Please guide me in my destiny
And help my dreams come true.
I believe I can do anything,
And though I've just begun,
Help me follow my dreams,
Not give up, and have a lot of fun.

Amen

I Can Make a Difference

Lord, it's important to keep our world clean and green.
One great way that I can help is by recycling.
Like juice boxes, bottles, newspapers, too.
They all can be made into something new.
Please help me to remember before I toss away,
I can make a difference by recycling every day.

Amen

Wise Words

Words can make you feel happy.
Some can make you sad.
A word spoken in anger
Can make you feel quite bad.
I pray that all the words I speak
On any given day
Are kind and thoughtful wise words,
At school, at home, or play.

Amen

A Thankful Heart

Lord, I really do like water
In all forms and shapes.
Oceans, rivers, waterfalls,
Puddles, ponds, and lakes.
I like rain, snow, and hail
Pouring down from the sky,
Water fountains, swimming pools,
Sprinklers squirting high.
May I always have a thankful heart
For all this splashing fun.
The world is like a water park
You made for everyone.

   Amen

Take Time to Pray

Lord, when I wake up, go to school,
Or have to take a bath,
In a hurry, running late,
Or working hard on math,
If my day is going slow,
Or filled with things to do,
I really like taking time
To talk and pray with you.
No matter what I'm doing
I know you always care.
Please help me to remember
The awesome power of prayer.

Amen

SUNSHINE MEADOWS

Meet the smart, funny friends
of Sunshine Meadows!

The Noble King Global
World traveling geography genius
and space explorer.

Miss Henny Twirl Henniford
Sweet, mannerly southern belle
and mama hen to all!

Rooster Tex Ranger
High-tech safety hero and protector
of Sunshine Meadows.

The Royal Schoolhouse Mouse
A very wise and merry mouse, and his wife,

Queen Serena
A prima ballerina.

Miss Sunny
Super smart teacher and computer whiz.

Professor Piggly Von Ziggly Swinestein
The most scientific pig of all time.

Theodeous Smithsonious
A brilliant, brainy bookworm with
a worm-a-graphic memory.

Mr. Happy Time
A time traveling talking clock, and

Edgar, the Eager Eagle
his pop-out-of-the-hat friend!

Learn to draw with
Uncle Rammy Ramwah,

and his tag-along niece,
Little Lamby.

Smarty-Sea-Saurus
Sunshine Meadows' very own
Smart-Ness Monster.

Yabbit the Rabbit
A very good friend to know!

Recyclo Jo
The most efficient Trash Transformer
with a cool quirky look!

The Ant Stooges
A wild and crazy bunch of ants.

Captain Joey, Scout Sergeant Curly Whirly,
and Sister Zoey.

Roarry
The story bear.

SUNSHINE MEADOWS

The sky's the limit!

Made in the USA
Charleston, SC
29 November 2012